DR. JIM
& THE SPECIAL
STETHOSCOPE

Story © 2010 by Scott Thomas Nicol
Illustrations © 2010 by David W. Youngblood

ISBN: 9780983035572

Creative House Kids Press
CreativeHousePress.com

A child is the light that guides you through whatever you feel is your journey. This book is dedicated to the guiding lights in my life, my beautiful children; *Amanda, Stephen and Brandon*. They provide me with wonderful challenges and a greater purpose. I love them with all my heart and all my soul.
Scott Thomas Nicol.

David W. Youngblood's Dedication
I would like to dedicate this book to the loving memory of my Grandparents, and in honor of my parents whose support, love and guidance have brought me to this point in my life.
I love them all dearly and thank them for everything.
I do not now know where I would be without them.

DR. JIM &
THE SPECIAL
STETHOSCOPE

Story by Scott Thomas Nicol
Illustrations by David W. Youngblood

Dr. Jim is a vet in a small country town
known as Polestock,
where residents had nary a frown.

They trusted this good man with their precious pets,

Treating ailments and small pains until the sun sets.

His clinic was located on the town's center square,
between Mildred's Fur Mufflers
and Joan's Outerwear.

Across from his clinic was a terrific fudge shop,

Where the people of Polestock were likely to stop.

Dr. Jim came to work, like he does every day,

to prepare for appointments in his own special way.

He put out the 'open' sign and welcome mat,

for his patients: a dog, a bird, rabbit and cat.

A knock on the door let Dr. Jim know

that his patients were anxious to see him, and so

they lined up from the front door
and 'round the next block.
Why were they so happy to see this fine doc?

See, the animals of Polestock, and this part is true,

knew something Polestocker's wished that they knew.

Dr. Jim's special stethoscope let him hear their ails,

from fleas and skin fungus to bothersome scales.

His stethoscope looked ordinary
from all points of view,
but this one was different,
it gave him a clue.

During each pets' exam, the animals would find
that this instrument would help
him to read each one's mind.

Dr. Jim's first patient, a black Persian cat,

who was not very happy with her face (it was flat).

"You're a Persian, you're beautiful!"
the doctor would say.
Satisfied the Persian cat went on her way.

A rabbit showed up from his hut on a farm,

worried someone wanted his foot for a charm.

Dr. Jim said, "You have four, how lucky is that?

Be thankful you don't have a face that is flat."

A parakeet was next on the doctor's check list,

bothered because she had never been kissed.

He picked her up and planted one on her round head.

if it wasn't for feathers, her cheeks would be red.

A small pug came in and had his exam,

he pulled a muscle while chasing a ram.

The vet wrapped him up and prescribed bed rest.

His shepherd skills must wait to be put to the test.

A bullfrog and lizard were next to be seen.

Walk-ins were part of the daily routine.

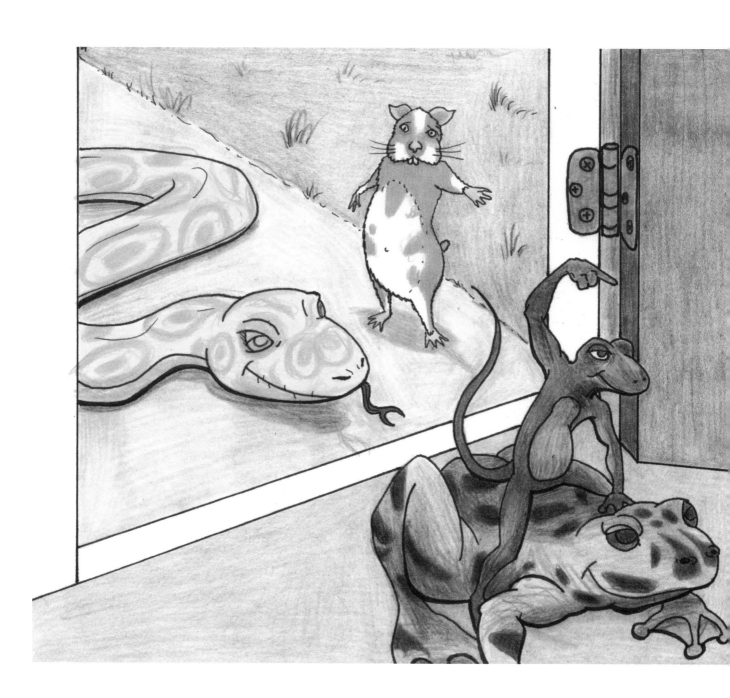

A hamster then snake followed them through the door.

Dr. Jim's stethoscope brought them in by the score.

This instrument had powers to discover all ills.

The doctor it pleases, the patients it thrills.

Dr. Jim was well known, from the east to the west.

As stethoscopes go, this one was the best.

One by one, pet by pet, day in and day out,

Dr. Jim would discover each animals' bout

with their problems,
regardless how big or how small,
whether this one's too tiny or that one's too tall.

The doctor, with stethoscope firmly in hand,

Left his patients in good health, all feeling grand.

He finished his day's work and locked the front door.

Knowing tomorrow had more patients in store.

DR. JIM's WORD CORNER

ailment (noun) – a physical disorder or illness, especially of a minor or chronic nature

anxious (adjective) – eager; earnestly desirous

bothersome (adjective) – causing annoyance; troublesome

bout (noun) – period or session; spell

clinic (noun) – a medical place for the treatment of non-residential patients

fungus (noun) – a spongy, abnormal growth formed on the skin

fur muffler (noun) – a scarf made from fur and worn around the neck for warmth

grand (adjective) – magnificent or splendid

DR. JIM's WORD CORNER

nary (adjective) – not any; no; never

ordinary (adjective) – of no special quality; common; plain

outerwear (noun) – garments, as raincoats or jackets, worn over clothing for warmth or protection

prescribe (verb) – to lay down rules; direct

routine (noun) – a customary or regular course of procedure or action

score (noun) – a great many

shepherd (verb) – to watch over; tend to or guard

stethoscope (noun) – an instrument used to convey sounds in the body to the ear of the examiner

Scott Thomas Nicol

Scott T. Nicol was born and raised in New Jersey. Although he doesn't write for a living (he works in the construction industry), he has always loved writing. "I would relish writing assignments in school. Even in college, I took creative writing courses as electives."

The *Dr. Jim* series of books he is creating, starting with *Dr. Jim & the Special Stethoscope*, has been something he considered doing for years. "I started fooling around with rhyming words and stanzas to tell this story. Finally, I got serious about it and created a cute concept about a young country veterinarian and this magical instrument he uses to figure out his patients' ills. It became a great little story. And in the subsequent stories are (and will be) as well. These could be a feature animated film in the making!"

Scott is married and has three beautiful children. "This whole story writing is, kind of, for them. I created these cute stories with them in mind."

David W. Youngblood

"Hey…"

David was born in Norman, Oklahoma, but was raised, for the most part, in Durham, North Carolina.

He studied "Fine Art" at both Louisburg College and at East Carolina University. However, his passion for Comic Books took him to New Jersey. David enrolled in The Joe Kubert School of Cartoon And Graphic Art, Inc., where his studies were completed upon his three years there. David shouts out a "Hello" to his fellow Kubie's!!

David has always enjoyed making people smile, through jokes, or by leaving sketches on people's desk, as they were away for lunch. But now, with the printing of *Dr. Jim and the Special Stethoscope*, David hopes to bring smiles to more people than just his family, friends and co-workers. God has given him a "gift". And now, he has given David the opportunity to use it and he greatly appreciates that, as this book almost didn't happen. Back in 2007, David's "gift" for drawing was taken away from him, though briefly, by a severe blow to his head. After many years, David was blessed to get his "gift" back. And now, he looks forward to what else lies ahead of him.